S0-BAZ-065

dw

MY SCHOOL, YOUR SCHOOL

For David and Hannah

Drawings by Susan Greene, Maria Pia Marrella and Debrah Welling

Cover Photo: Ted Horowitz/The Stock Market

Pages 4–5 Michael Heron; pages 6–7 Lawrence Migdale; pages 8–9 Richard Hutchings; pages 10–17 Lawrence Migdale; pages 18–19 Lea/Omni-Photo Communications; pages 20–21 Michal Heron; pages 22–23 Ted Horowitz/The Stock Market.

First Steck-Vaughn Edition 1992

Copyright © 1990 American Teacher Publications

Published by Steck-Vaughn Company

All rights reserved. No part of the material protected by this copyright may be reproduced or utilized in any form by any means, electronic or mechanical, including photocopying, recording, or by any information storage and retrieval system, without permission in writing from Steck-Vaughn Company, P.O. Box 26015, Austin, TX 78755. Printed in the United States of America.

Library of Congress number: 89-70338

Library of Congress Cataloging in Publication Data.

Birnbaum, Bette.
   My school, your school / by Bette Birnbaum.

   (Ready-set-read)
   Summary: A photo essay that follows young children through a typical school day. The text invites the readers to compare their school experiences with the narrators'.
   [1. Schools—Fiction.] I. Title. II. Series.
   PZ7.B5228My   1990   [E]—dc20   89-70338

ISBN 0-8172-3583-3   hardcover library binding

ISBN 0-8114-6743-0   softcover binding

         5 6 7 8 9   96 95 94 93 92

My School, Your School

by Bette Birnbaum

E
BIRN

MONGER SCHOOL LIBRARY
Elkhart, Indiana

RSVP
RAINTREE
STECK-VAUGHN
P U B L I S H E R S
The Steck-Vaughn Company

Austin, Texas

Here I am at my school.
That's me at my desk, saying
good morning to my teacher.
My teacher's name is Mrs. Siegal.

What is your teacher's name?

Here I am at my school.
That's me saying "O." My teacher is
playing an alphabet game with us.

What games do you play in school?

Here I am at my school.
That's me and Billy with a shape
puzzle. We like working together.
We are best friends.

Who are your friends at school?

Here I am at my school.
That's me writing a story at the computer.
I like to write stories about dinosaurs.

What do you like to write about?

Here I am at my school.
That's me in the middle circle. After lunch
I like to play in the school yard with my friends.

12

What do you like
to do after lunch?

Here I am at my school.
That's me coloring in my math workbook.
Math is what I like to do best at school.

What do you like to
do best at school?

Here I am at my school.
That's me playing the maracas.
For music we usually sing songs,
but today we are playing instruments.

16

What does your class do for music?

Here I am at my school.
That's me in the wolf costume.
Can you guess what play we are putting on?
Putting on plays is one of the special things
we do at school.

What special things do you do at school?

Here I am at my school.
That's me reading a book to my friends.
Sometimes we read at the end of the day.

When do you read books in school?

Here I am after school.
That's me with my friend Tasha at the
bus stop across the street from my house.
My mom is waiting for us.
I can't wait to tell her all about my day!

What will you tell about your day?

Sharing the Joy of Reading

Reading a book aloud to your child is just one way you can help your child experience the joy of reading. Now that you and your child have shared **My School, Your School,** you can help your child begin to think and react as a reader by encouraging him or her to:

- Retell or reread the story with you, looking and listening for the repetition of specific letters, sounds, words, or phrases.

- Make a picture of a favorite character, event, or key concept from this book.

- Talk about his or her own ideas and feelings about the subject of this book and other things he or she might want to know about this subject.

Here is an activity that you can do together to help extend your child's appreciation of this book: You and your child can discuss school experiences. Talk with your child about his or her school friends, the classroom teacher, and school activities. Then tell about your own school days. You can each make a picture to help compare your different school experiences.